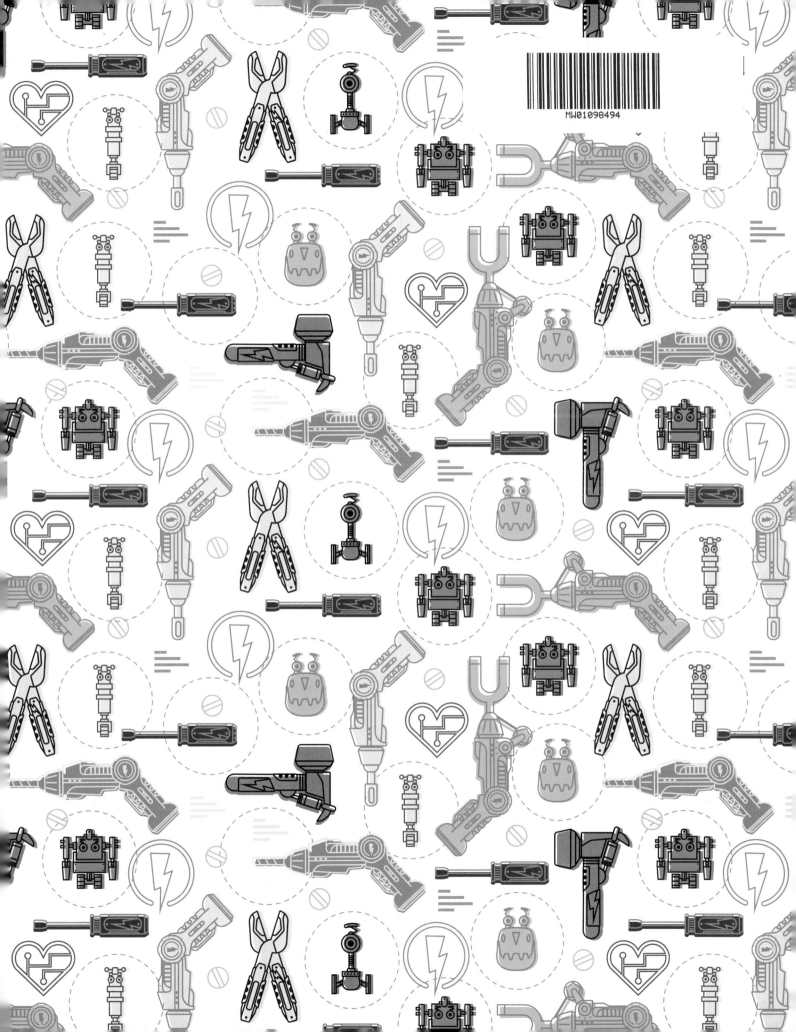

WILD WINTER ADVENTURE!

Adapted by **STEVE BEHLING**

Based on the teleplay "Rusty's Ski Trip Blip"
by Dustin Ferrer

Illustrated by **MJ ILLUSTRATIONS**

 A GOLDEN BOOK · NEW YORK

randomhousekids.com
ISBN 978-1-5247-2067-4
Printed in the United States of America
10 9 8 7 6 5 4 3 2 1

It was a bright, sunny day, and Rusty was busy with a new project in the Recycling Yard.

"Just one more screw," he said as he revved up his TurboTool screwdriver.

VRRRRRRT! VRRRRRRT!

Botasaur burst out laughing when Rusty began to attach a boot to his robotic foot.

"Wow, for somebody so big, you sure are ticklish!" giggled Rusty.

Rusty finished attaching two huge metal ski boots to Botasaur's feet.

"Operation Dino Boot Build is complete!" he cheered.

Botasaur was so happy, he gave Rusty a big LICK!

"Whoa!" said Rusty. "Thanks, buddy. I'm glad you like them!"

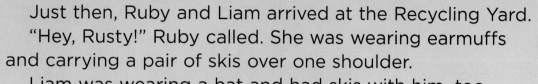

Just then, Ruby and Liam arrived at the Recycling Yard.

"Hey, Rusty!" Ruby called. She was wearing earmuffs and carrying a pair of skis over one shoulder.

Liam was wearing a hat and had skis with him, too. "Ready to go skiing?" he asked Rusty.

"Am I ever!" answered Rusty. He pointed to a pair of enormous skis, each one with a big jet engine on it. "I can't wait to try out these all-new, turbo-powered, high-speed, dual-throttle INCREDO-SKIS!"

Ruby looked at the Incredo-Skis. They *were* incredible . . .
and also pretty HUGE!

"Aren't they a little big for you?" she asked.

"For me?" answered Rusty. "Way too big. But for
Botasaur, they're perfect! Go ahead, Botasaur—try them on!"

Botasaur let out a happy roar and stepped onto the skis.

SNAP! SNAP! The skis snapped onto his boots. The
playful robot dino loved them!

Botasaur couldn't wait to go skiing. He imagined what it would be like to soar down a snowy mountain on the Incredo-Skis.
SHOOSH! SHOOSH! SHOOSH!
Lost in his imagination, Botasaur pretended to ski—a little too hard. "Look out!" cried Rusty as Botasaur's tail sailed over his head.

The tail landed on the ground with a loud CRASH.
"Note to self," said Rusty, "check Botasaur's tail alignment!"
Ruby pulled out her tablet and tapped the screen. "Don't
worry," she told Botasaur. "We'll get some Bits on the fix!"

Inside the Rivet Lab, the Bits' station whirred to life.
One by one, out popped Ray, Crush, Whirly, and Jack!

"Guys!" Ruby announced. "Tail emergency!"

The Bits went to work. Ray shined his light on Botasaur so Rusty could see what he was doing. Crush, Whirly, and Jack picked up Botasaur's tail. Then Rusty bolted it into place.

"All right, buddy. Give it a test wag!" said Rusty.

Botasaur wagged his tail a little. It worked! Then he gave it an even bigger wag. His tail was as good as new!

HONK! HONK!

Just then, a bright yellow school bus pulled up to the workshop. The doors opened, and out came Sammy Scoops!

"Hey, guys!" he said cheerfully. "Who's ready to hit the slopes?"

Everyone grabbed their gear and raced onto the bus.

Rusty tapped a button on his glove. A big claw picked up Botasaur's skis and put them on top of the bus.

"TIME TO BOLT!" called Rusty.

Botasaur was too big to fit on the bus, but he
had no trouble keeping up.
His giant footsteps shook the whole street!

The bus left town and headed up the mountain with Botasaur following. Up, up, up they went. Ruby looked out the bus window. She couldn't believe how high up they were! Liam sat with Crush and Ray. They were excited for all the snow.

"We're almost at Planner's Peak, guys!" said Rusty. "Nothing can stop us now!"

And that was when the bus screeched to a sudden STOP!

"Well," said Sammy. "Maybe *that* will stop us."
Everyone peered out the front window.
"Whoa!" said Rusty. "That's one huge sinkhole!"

"I've got an idea," said Ruby. "Whirly? Let's see if there's another way to Planner's Peak."

Whirly flew high into the air.

With a tap on her tablet, Ruby loaded Whirly's WhirlyCam program. Everything Whirly saw appeared on Ruby's screen.

Ruby sighed. "This is the only road for miles."

Sammy hung his head. "And just like that, our ski trip is over faster than two scoops of ice cream in a pizza oven."

Sammy was sad, but Botasaur was even sadder. He really
wanted to use his Incredo-Skis! He let out a whimper.

"Aw, don't be sad, Botasaur," said Rusty. "We'll figure out
a way to get this trip back on track!"

"But how?" asked Ruby.

"With those!" Rusty exclaimed, pointing to the Incredo-Skis
on top of the bus.

Rusty knew who could help him put his plan into action: Jack. His robot buddy quickly measured the Incredo-Skis to make sure they were as wide as the wheels of the bus, then placed them over the sinkhole.

"Thanks, Jack," said Ruby. "The skis make a perfect bridge. Next stop, the mountaintop!"

Everyone boarded the bus again. Sammy slowly started across the skis. The skis went **CREAK! CREAK! MOAN!** but they held strong.

"We're gonna make it!" shouted Rusty.

Everyone cheered when the bus made it to the other side. Botasaur was so happy, he jumped for joy.

"Oh, no!" cried Liam. "That huge rock is going to fall!"

Rusty looked up and saw a boulder. Botasaur was jumping so hard, it was making the boulder move back and forth!

"Botasaur—down, boy!" he called.

THUMP! THUMP!

Botasaur stopped jumping, and the boulder stopped moving. Rusty told Botasaur to cross over to the bus. Botasaur put a ski in his mouth, then slowly crossed the sinkhole along the other ski. "That's it," Rusty whispered. "Good job. Nice and easy . . ."

Botasaur got to the other side! He was so happy, he didn't notice a tiny pebble in front of him until he tripped over it and hit the ground with a big **BOOM**!

The ground shook. The boulder above them rumbled and tumbled and . . .

. . . **SMASHED**!

The big boulder crashed to the road in front of the bus.

"This might be a little problem," Rusty said.

Ruby took a look at the boulder and sighed. "That thing's not going anywhere."

But Rusty had an idea. Maybe Botasaur could use his strength to move the boulder!

Botasaur pushed. He shoved. But the boulder wouldn't budge.

Rusty tried to think of another idea. "What if we use Botasaur's Incredo-Skis again?" he asked.

Liam thought that was a great idea. "Is there anything these skis *can't* do?" he asked.

Botasaur put one ski beneath the boulder. Then he stomped on the ski. Nothing. He jumped on the ski again. Nothing. Then he **LEAPED** onto the ski! The boulder stayed still, but Botasaur went Bota-*soaring* into the sky!

"Are you okay?" called Ruby.

She heard a whimper from way up high. Botasaur poked his head out from behind the boulder. He was fine, but the boulder was still blocking the road.

"I think our ski trip is officially canceled," Sammy sighed.

"If only we could fly like Botasaur did," said Liam, "we could get over that rock in no time."

"Fly? Hold on a second!" said Rusty.

"You know what would be really, really, really cool?" asked Rusty.

"Ice cream?" answered Sammy.

"Skiing?" suggested Liam.

"Skiing on ice cream?" said Sammy excitedly.

Ruby laughed. "All awesome ideas, but . . ."

"Ruby and I have an idea to help us get over that rock!" Rusty said.

"Let's combine it and design it!" Rusty and Ruby said together. Using his Utility Glove, Rusty drew a blueprint in the air. He and Ruby started to plan.

Then Rusty and his friends went to work. Jack hoisted Botasaur's Incredo-Skis onto the roof of the bus.

Rusty attached a thick steel cable to one of Botasaur's ski poles. Next, they attached Botasaur's tail to their creation.

Ruby fastened two big engines to each end of one of the skis. Whirly tightened the screws into place.

"MODIFIED. CUSTOMIZED. RUSTIFIED!"

said Rusty as they snapped the last piece into place.
He turned to his friends. "Introducing . . .

". . . the Awesome School-Bus-Copter 4000!" he said.

Rusty was right—it *was* awesome! They had combined Botasaur's tail, the Incredo-Skis, and Sammy's bus to make a flying bus. They could use it to fly over the boulder to the top of the mountain!

"It looks like this ski trip is officially back on!" Sammy said with a smile. "Time to jet!"

They were ready to go skiing at last!

With the touch of a few buttons on Rusty's Utility Glove, the Awesome School-Bus-Copter 4000 came to life. Engines hummed. Turbines whirred. Helicopter blades began to spin. Soon the bus was in the air!

The flying bus rose up, up, up, until it was above the boulder.

"All right!" said Rusty. "Let's give Botasaur a lift, too!"
He pressed another button on his glove, and a claw came out
of the bottom of the flying bus. "Okay, boy. Up!"
   Botasaur jumped as high as he could. The claw caught him!
"Punch it, Sammy!" said Rusty.

Sammy pushed the throttle on the Awesome School-Bus-Copter 4000, and off they went.

"I'm flying!" Sammy shouted. "I'm as free as a bird!" In his excitement, he flew the bus in a big upside-down loop!

Sammy gulped. "Maybe I'll just be a bird that flies in a straight line from now on."

Just then, Liam looked down and gasped. "Oh, no!" he said. "How is that car going to get across?"

On the mountain road below, a car had skidded to a stop. The sinkhole was blocking its way, too!

Rusty gave Liam a reassuring smile. "Don't worry," he said. "I built in a little extra surprise to help clear the road!"

Rusty touched the button on his Utility Glove once more.

A cable fired from the back of the bus. Ruby shook her head. "You made a grappling hook out of Botasaur's ski pole?"

"Of course!" laughed Rusty. "Every Awesome School-Bus-Copter 4000 needs a grappling hook!"

The hook sank into the boulder.

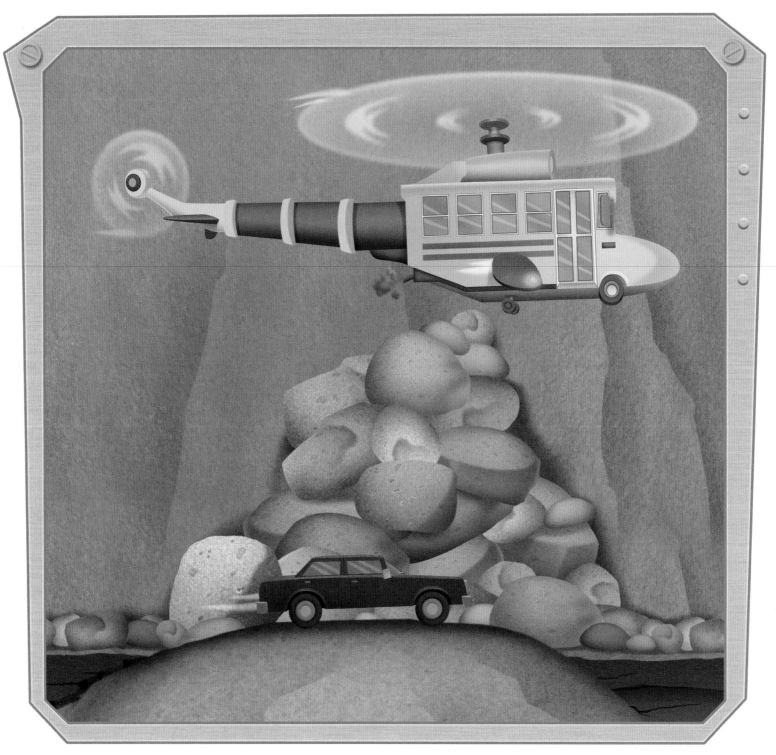

The engines whined as the Awesome School-Bus-Copter 4000 strained to hoist the heavy boulder. But inch by inch, the giant rock was dragged closer to the sinkhole!

Finally, with one last pull, the boulder fell into the sinkhole, filling it in perfectly. The road was safe again! The driver of the car honked the horn to thank Rusty.

"Now let's hit the slopes!" shouted Rusty, and everyone cheered.

Soon the Awesome School-Bus-Copter 4000 landed at the top of Planner's Peak.

While Sammy grabbed his snowboard, Rusty, Ruby, and Liam put Botasaur's tail back where it belonged. Then the friends took the skis off the Awesome School-Bus-Copter 4000 and snapped them onto Botasaur's feet.

"All right!" shouted Sammy as he zipped by. "Race you guys to the bottom!"

"Okay," said Rusty. "You ready to do this, Botasaur?"

Botasaur let out a happy roar. Everyone hopped onto his back—
Rusty, Ruby, Liam, and even the Bits!

"Let's see what these skis can do!" shouted Rusty. The engines on
the skis started to rumble. Rusty and his friends held on tight as
Botasaur took off down the mountain after Sammy. **WHOOSH!**

Botasaur's skis worked better than Rusty had hoped!
They all flew down the side of the mountain, bouncing off the snow.
"Best. Ski trip. Ever!" shouted Liam.
"Woo-hoo!" yelled Rusty and Ruby.

In no time at all, they spotted Sammy snowboarding just ahead.
Botasaur rocketed right past him, spraying snow everywhere.
A pile of snow fell on Sammy, turning him into a human snowman!

WHUMP!

Sammy's head popped out of the snow. "Wow. Now I know what a snow cone feels like!" he said.

Everyone laughed. It really *was* the best ski trip ever!

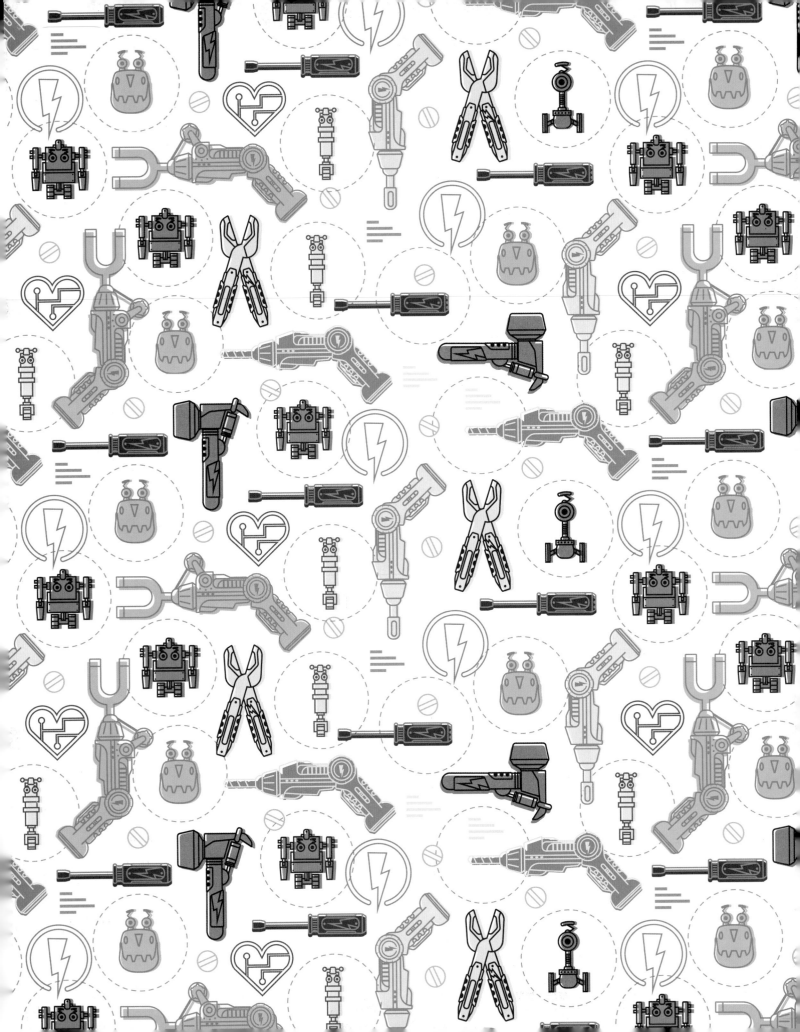